TITCHY WITCH

AND THE BIRTHDAY BROOMSTICK

For Kaia
R.I.

To Nick
K.M.

ORCHARD BOOKS
338 Euston Road, London NW1 3BH
Orchard Books Australia
Level 17/207 Kent Street, Sydney, NWS 2000
First published in Great Britain in 2003
First paperback publication in 2004
This edition published in 2015
ISBN 978 1 40833 771 4
Text © Rose Impey 2003 Illustrations © Katharine McEwen 2003
The rights of Rose Impey to be identified as the author and
Katharine McEwen to be identified as the illustrator of this Work
have been asserted by them in accordance with the
Copyright, Designs and Patents Act, 1988.
A CIP catalogue record for this book is available from the British Library
1 3 5 7 9 10 8 6 4 2
Printed in China
Orchard Books is a division of Hachette Children's Books,
an Hachette UK company
www.hachette.co.uk

TITCHY WITCH

AND THE BIRTHDAY BROOMSTICK

ROSE IMPEY ★ KATHARINE McEWEN

ORCHARD

Titchy-witch woke up, itchy-scratchy with excitement. Today she was seven witch-years old.

She peeped in on Mum and
Dad, but they were still asleep.

Weeny-witch was still asleep too.

Cat-a-bogus opened one eye, then closed it again.

Even Eric was still dozing.

So Titchy-witch
went to watch
for the post. Mr P
flew in with four
parcels.

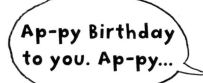

8

Titchy-witch grabbed the biggest
parcel and opened it.
Her first broomstick!
Titchy-witch jumped on and
held tight.

But nothing happened.
Mr P squawked with
laughter. Titchy-witch gave
him a little witchy stare.

She didn't know much magic yet,
but she was sure she could turn
him into a turnip, if she tried.

Now Mum and Dad were up,
Titchy-witch wanted to learn
to fly, this minute.

But Witchy-witch and Wendel were
off to work.

"Cat-a-bogus will show you," they
called. And they disappeared in a
swirl of dust.

Cat-a-bogus had better things to do, but he did like showing off.

"We'll start with a few rules," he hissed.

"Number one: no flying outside."
"Yes, yes," said Titchy-witch.

"Number two: hold on with
both hands."
"Yes, yes, yes," said Titchy-witch.

"Number three: no standing up!"
Standing up! Titchy-witch hadn't
even thought of that!

At last Cat-a-bogus told her the magic words.

"Zig-a-zag-a-zoom, fly this broomstick round the room!"

But, even with the magic
words, flying wasn't easy.
Titchy-witch kept sliding off.

Or bumping into things.

Bang! Smash! She crashed
into the ceiling.

"Dive!" growled Cat-a-bogus.

So Titchy-witch dived.

And, suddenly, she was flying.

"I can fly!" she squealed.

"Watch me! Watch me!"

But the cat had better things
to do than watch a little witch.
He left Titchy-witch giving
Victor a ride.

All day, they flew round the house,
until Victor felt quite dizzy.
"Flying's easy-breezy," said
Titchy-witch.

She thought it was *so* easy,
she started to break the rules.

Then Titchy-witch broke the most important rule. She opened the window and flew outside!

"Zig-a-zag-a-zoom, fly this broomstick out of this room!"

Oh, dear!

23

The broomstick zoomed over
the roof of the house.
It flew so fast it almost hit
the chimney.

Now Titchy-witch felt dizzy too.
She wanted to stop, but she
didn't know how to.

It was getting dark. Suddenly,
something came flying towards
her. It was Witchy-witch,
hurrying home.

She had to swerve to miss
Titchy-witch. And *something* fell
off the back of her broomstick.

Down...

down...

down...it fell.

But Titchy-witch knew what to do.
She dived down, just in time to
catch Weeny-witch.

The baby squealed with delight. She liked flying too.

Because it was her birthday,
Mum and Dad weren't too
cross with Titchy-witch.
They had a special birthday tea.

Maggots and mash!
And beetle juice jelly for afters!

That night, Titchy-witch went to
sleep hugging her broomstick,
and dreaming about flying.

TITCHY WITCH

BY ROSE IMPEY ILLUSTRATED BY KATHARINE McEWEN

Enjoy a little more magic with all the Titchy-witch tales:

Orchard Books are available from all good
bookshops, or can be ordered from our website:
www.orchardbooks.co.uk
or telephone 01235 827702, or fax 01235 827703.

Prices and availability are subject to change.

Race Ahead with Reading

Stone Age Adventures

Little Nut's Lucky Escape

By Vivian French

Illustrated by Cate James

W

The Stone Age Family

Pod

Pim

Little Nut

Dada Boulder

Old Boulder

Chapter One

The bushes were scratchy and the
wind was cold.

"Carry!" demanded Little Nut.

"No," Pod told him.

Little Nut began to cry.

3

"I'll carry you, little brother," Pim said.

"Don't," said Pod. "He's a nuisance. Why does he have to come with us anyway? He's too small and too slow."

Old Boulder swung Little Nut onto his huge

shoulders. "Little Nut needs to learn.

Big ones hunt while little ones look for

berries with the old ones."

"I'm nearly big," Pod said crossly,
"and I can run fast. What if we get
attacked by a bear?" Pim looked worried.
"A bear? Are there b-b-bears round here?"

Old Boulder smiled at her. "What's the rule, Pim?" Pim smiled back. "Look for danger, listen for danger and smell for danger wherever you are."

Pod pulled at Old Boulder's arm. "Do we HAVE to look for berries?" he asked.

"Yes," Big Boulder growled. "Do as you're told."

Pod sighed, but he didn't ask any more questions. Old Boulder had once killed a wolf all by himself. You don't annoy someone who kills wolves, even if they are very, very old and sleep a lot!

Chapter Two

"Look!" Pim had found a berry bush.

"Make sure you only pick the ripe ones.

Don't eat them!" Old Boulder said as he

dropped Little Nut onto the ground, before

plonking himself down under a tree.

"My poor old bones need a rest," he said.
"Pod, you look after Little Nut. Off you go.
And don't come back until your baskets are
full." Pim looked at her reed basket. It
suddenly looked very big.

"Full to the very top?" she asked.

"Full to the very top." Old Boulder gave a
huge yawn. "Everyone works, everyone eats.
Nobody works, everyone goes hungry. And
we don't want to go hungry tonight."

"Why?" Pod wanted to know. "Is someone coming?" Old Boulder shut his eyes.

"Wait and see," he said, then started to snore.

Pod, Pim and Little Nut looked round. There were plenty of bushes, but the little blue berries were hidden under the leaves, and hard to find. Pim shook her head. "It'll take AGES to fill the baskets," she sighed.

Pod grinned. "I know how to get the baskets full in no time." Pim and Little Nut looked at him hopefully. "If we fill the baskets with stones," Pod explained, "all we have to do is pick just enough berries to cover them up."

Chapter Three

"Won't Old Boulder be cross?" Pim asked.
Pod shrugged. "He won't know. He doesn't
do the cooking." But Pim didn't agree.
"I'm going to pick real berries," she said.
"Berries," repeated Little Nut, and he picked
up his basket hungrily.

Pod stuck out his tongue. "Goody-goody!"

"Don't care," Pim told him, and she began peering under the leaves of the berry bushes. Pod turned his back on her, and began picking up stones. He put some in the basket, but the smooth and round ones he put into his deerskin pouch.

"If I climb the tree I can throw them at the birds," he told himself. "Old Boulder won't think I'm a baby if I kill a juicy gull for supper." Pod finished long before Pim.

He put his basket beside Big Boulder, and began to climb the tree. From the top he could see over the hill, and he rubbed his eyes and stared. "Uh-oh! There's smoke coming from the village!" He waved at Pim, and shouted, "Pim! PIM!"

Old Boulder sat up with a grunt and grabbed his spear. "What? What is it?"

"They've started cooking," Pod told him.

"There must be visitors!" Pim came running.

"What is it? Is there danger?"

"Only from this silly boy," Old Boulder said.

"It's time to go home. Where's Little Nut?"

19

Pim looked up at Pod, and Pod stared wildly round. "I can't see him..."

Old Boulder jumped up with a roar.

"YOU CAN'T SEE HIM?" Pod began to tremble. "I'm sorry—"

"Stay there. Keep looking!" Old Boulder heaved himself to his feet and put his fingers in his mouth. His ear-splitting whistle made Pim jump.

On the other side of the hill, Pod's father seized his weapons ... and the uncles seized theirs too.

Chapter Four

As the men came hurrying, Old Boulder picked up Pim and went to meet them. Pod felt sick. Was Little Nut lost forever? He peered at the ground below, squinting at something moving in the bushes.

WHAT WAS THAT? Pod slid down the tree. In and out of the bushes he ran, careless of the thorns, until he found Little Nut, fast asleep inside his empty basket.

There, munching the last of Little Nut's berries was a wild boar.

Pod took a deep breath. The boar was old, and scraggy, but it was grunting angrily and its tusks were long and sharp. In the distance Pod could hear shouting. The boar heard the noise as well, and it looked up –

"GET AWAY FROM MY LITTLE BROTHER!" Pod yelled. He seized his leather pouch full of stones, swung it round and round his head – and let go. WHACK! The bag hit the wild boar right between the eyes.

Chapter Five

"UMPH!" The boar staggered back with a
loud grunt. Pod reached for Little Nut's arm
just as his father came bursting into view.

As Pod hauled Little Nut away, his father sprang at the boar with his spear. Seconds later it was dead, and there was a loud cheer from the uncles.

"What have you to say?" Old Boulder growled. Pod hung his head. "I didn't look after Little Nut ... and I didn't stay in the tree when you told me to ... and I filled my basket with stones and leaves underneath the berries."

The uncles began to laugh, but Old Boulder held up his hand. "No, Pod. You ran towards danger – that is very bad."

"But he saved his brother," the tallest uncle said. "AND he knocked out a wild boar!"

The tallest uncle rubbed his stomach.

"There'll be a really fine feast tonight."

"With lots of delicious berries?" asked Pod.

Pim nodded. Dada Boulder looked at Pod.

"Well, Pod, what do you say?" Pod thought

for a moment. Then he said:

"I think I did well ... in the end."

Life in the Stone Age

The Stone Age began around 2.6 million years ago. It was called the Stone Age as people used tools and weapons made of stone. Using sharp spears, they hunted wild animals like boar but had to avoid the lions, bears and woolly mammoths! They foraged in the wild for nuts and berries to eat. The ways people in the Stone Age found their food meant they became known as hunter-gatherers.

Franklin Watts
First published in Great Britain in 2015 by
The Watts Publishing Group

Text © Vivian French 2015
Illustrations © Cate James 2015

Series Editor: Melanie Palmer
Series Advisor: Catherine Glavina
Series Designers: Peter Scoulding
and Cathryn Gilbert

ISBN 978 1 4451 4127 5 (hbk)
ISBN 978 1 4451 4130 5 (pbk)
ISBN 978 1 4451 4129 9 (library ebook)

Printed in China

MIX
Paper from
responsible sources

FSC
www.fsc.org
FSC® C104740

Franklin Watts
An imprint of
Hachette Children's Group
Part of The Watts Publishing Group
Carmelite House
50 Victoria Embankment
London EC4Y 0DZ

An Hachette UK Company
www.hachette.co.uk

www.franklinwatts.co.uk